D1624116

# HOCUS POCUS HOTEL

Hocus Pocus Hotel is published by Stone Arch Books
A Capstone Imprint
1710 Roe Crest Dr.
North Mankato, Minnesota 56003
www.capstonepub.com

Cataloging-in-Publication Data is available at the Library
of Congress website.

ISBN: 978-1-4342-4101-6 (library binding)

Summary: A volunteer assistant vanishes during a trick
at the Abracadabra. Can Tyler and Charlie make him
appear?

Photo credits: Shutterstock
Abracadabra Hotel Illustration: Brann Garvey
Designed by Kay Fraser

Printed in China
092012
006934LEOS13

# The Assistant Vanishes!

BY MICHAEL DAHL

ILLUSTRATED BY LISA K. WEBER

 STONE ARCH BOOKS™

a capstone imprint

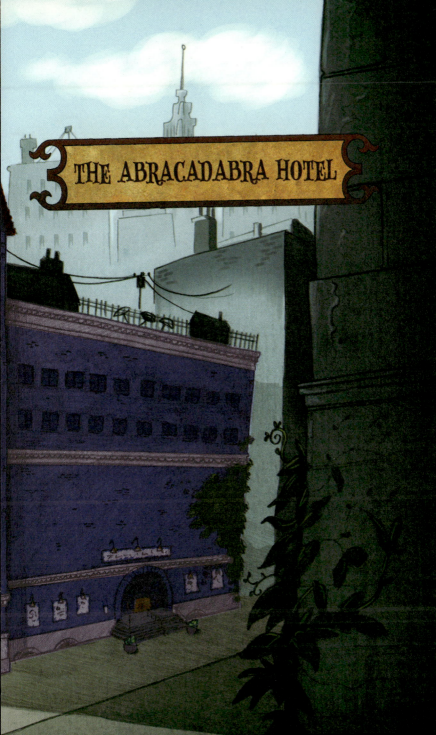

Table of

# Contents

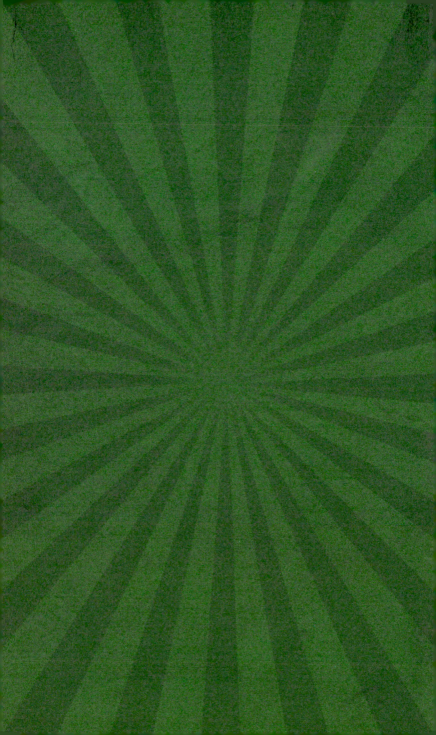

# The Premiere

On Friday at three o'clock, just after the bell rang, Tyler Yu and Charlie Hitchcock stood together inside the back doors of Blackstone Middle School.

Each of them clutched a packet of bright yellow paper.

All around them, other students took books from their lockers, packed their bags, and made plans for the weekend.

It was an ordinary Friday afternoon. There was nothing at all unusual about the scene.

Except that Ty was the biggest bully in school, and Charlie was best known for his photographic memory, and they weren't supposed to be friends.

"Okay," Ty said. "I think this is where we split up."

Charlie nodded.

"I'll hand out flyers to the eighth graders," Ty went on. "Then I'll hand out more flyers to the jocks, the cool kids, the cheerleaders, and the crew in detention."

"Who does that leave for me?" Charlie asked, looking up at Ty.

"The dorks," Ty said. He shrugged. "And the nerds."

Charlie rolled his eyes. "Don't forget the geeks."

"Them too," Ty agreed. He pointed toward the science wing. "You go that way."

"Obviously," Charlie said. He walked off into the crowd.

"And remember — you don't know me," Ty called after him.

Charlie reached the first corner and stopped. Then he turned and saw Ty, across the main hallway, handing some yellow sheets to two eighth-grade girls.

"I think they'll figure out that we know each other," Charlie hollered, "when they realize we're handing out the same flyers!"

Smiling, he headed down the science hallway.

He would never have tried something like that a few weeks ago, but ever since Charlie helped Ty solve two magic mysteries at the Abracadabra Hotel, the two boys had become something like friends.

Ty would probably deny that.

Actually, Charlie was sure Ty would deny that.

But he knew it was true.

Thirty minutes later, the boys met up at the front of the school. All the flyers were handed out, except one, which Charlie still held in both hands.

"You have one left," Ty said. "Did you give one to every kid?"

Charlie nodded.

"Chess club?" Ty asked.

"Yup," said Charlie.

"Computer club?" Ty asked.

"Of course," said Charlie.

"What about the chemistry club?" Ty suggested.

"Got 'em," Charlie said. "I promise. I got everyone. This one is to hang up."

Charlie led the way to the office bulletin board. He handed the flyer to Ty. "Hold this," he said. Then Charlie pulled two tacks from his pocket, took the flyer back from Ty, and tacked it into place on the bulletin board.

"There," Charlie said. The boys stood back and looked at the flyer.

The
# ABRACADABRA
## HOTEL

*is proud to present*

### ITS FIRST MAGIC SHOW IN FIFTY YEARS

## TWO SHOWS THIS SATURDAY
## 12 NOON AND 7 P.M.

## FEATURING

MADAME KRZYSCKY, THE FIRE-EATER
MIND-READING HYPNOTISM BY
THE GREAT PROFESSOR PONTIFICATE
THE AMAZING MR. THURSDAY, JUGGLER
AND ALL THE WAY FROM THE LOST KINGDOM OF GILJARRI . . .
EXPLORER OF MAGICAL REALMS . . . MASTER OF DIMENSIONAL POWERS
BEYOND YOUR WILDEST IMAGININGS . . .
THE GREATEST PERFORMER OF OUR AGE OR ANY AGE . . . .

## THE GREAT AND POWERFUL
# THEOPOLIS!

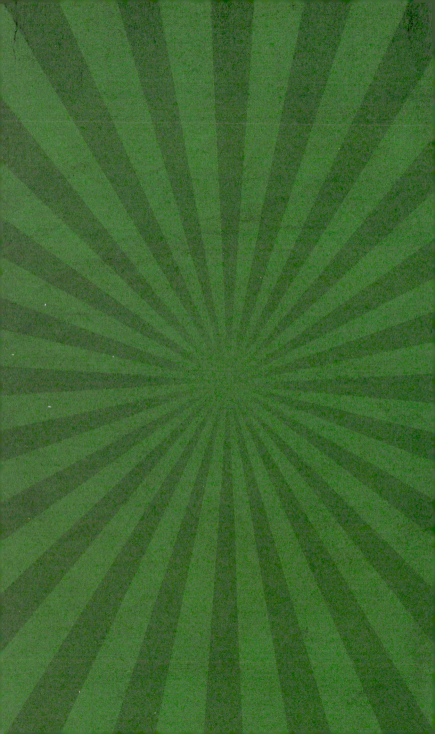

# Like New

Everyone at the Abracadabra Hotel had a job to do for the hotel's first magic show in decades.

Ty's job was to collect tickets.

Before the show started, he stood at the door to the old theater, wearing a maroon

tuxedo. He tugged at a tight collar. There were still a few minutes until show time.

"That's a good look for you," Charlie said, walking over. He wore a simple dark gray suit. Everyone attending would be dressed up, like people did in the old days when they went to the theater. Charlie sat down near Ty's door, on an old red velvet bench.

Everything in the old theater had been cleaned and refurbished for the big opening night. The bench looked like it had been made yesterday, even though it was almost sixty years old — as old as the hotel itself. Even the old carved Tragedy and Comedy faces on the theater's double doors had been perfectly polished.

Just then, Brack walked up.

"Hello, young gentlemen," he said.

Brack was the old elevator operator, but he had a secret too, a secret as old as the hotel itself. And Charlie was the first person to discover it.

Brack was actually Mr. Abracadabra, the founder and namesake of the hotel and one of the most famous magicians of all time. Charlie was the only one who knew.

Brack had organized this magic show. He wanted to bring the spotlight back to the Abracadabra Hotel for one last amazing show, but today's show wasn't the full spectacle he had in mind. It was a kind of dress rehearsal for the really big show.

Charlie couldn't wait. But in the meantime, he couldn't tell anyone that he knew Brack was anyone other than the elevator operator.

Today, Brack wasn't wearing his old-

fashioned elevator-operator uniform.
Instead, he was dressed to the nines, in a
tuxedo with tails, a top hat, and a cane.

Ty shook his head slowly. "That's not
fair," he grumbled quietly to Charlie. "Brack
gets to wear that cool tux, and I'm stuck
dressed like a couch."

Charlie chuckled. "Is it just about
showtime?" he asked.

The old man pulled a gold watch from
his pocket. It swung at the end of a long,
thin gold chain.

"Nice watch," Ty said.

"Thank you," Brack said, admiring the
antique. "It's older than this hotel. It's older
than I am. In fact, I don't know old it is."

Charlie tried to get a glimpse of the
watch as Brack twirled it on its chain.

"Would you like to see it?" Brack asked. He stopped it from swinging, caught it in his palm with a thump, and held it out to the boys.

"Thanks," Charlie said, grinning. He grabbed the watch. The chain was quite long. He held it between himself and Ty, so they could both get a look at it. When Ty hit a little button on top, the face swung open so they could see the time. The watch had exposed gears — it looked like dozens of them. It ticked and tocked loudly.

Two minutes to noon. The show was about to start.

"Thanks, Brack," Charlie said. He handed the watch back. "You better get to your seat."

"And you boys had better get inside too," Brack said, walking past them. "I don't think you'll want to miss this show."

The boys watched Brack walk down the long aisle toward his special box in the front.

"He's up to something," Ty said.

Charlie shrugged. "Of course he is," he said. "He always is."

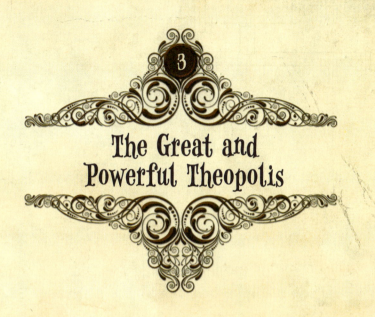

# The Great and Powerful Theopolis

Charlie and Ty headed into the darkening theater. Their seats were in the very front row of the balcony, where they could see almost the whole theater, though they were pretty far away from the stage.

The spotlight thumped on, pointing right at Brack in his special box. He stood up and waved. The crowd clapped.

"Ladies and gentlemen," Brack said, "and children of all ages! Welcome to the first performance of magic, illusion, and intrigue at Abracadabra Hotel in fifty years."

The crowd clapped and cheered. Charlie spotted a whole bunch of kids he recognized from school, all sitting in a group in the section behind Brack. The rest of the theater was sparsely filled, mostly with guests from the hotel.

"Enjoy the show," Brack said, and the spotlight switched off. The curtain went up, and the stage was lit.

The fire-eater was very exciting. The kids from Blackstone Middle School cheered and hollered when Madame Krzyscky swallowed a flaming sword as her grand finale.

Professor Pontificate, the mind reader and hypnotist, convinced one of the hotel guests that she was a chicken. For the rest of the show, the poor woman waddled around the theater saying, "Cluck, cluck!" and trying to eat worms from the floor.

Mr. Thursday had spent tons of time practicing, and it showed. His juggling act was wonderful. But everyone was waiting for the main attraction. Finally, it was time for the Great Theopolis of Giljarri!

The stage filled with smoke. A heavy black curtain closed across the middle of the stage, adding an air of gravity. Thunder clapped in the catwalks. Laughter — loud and dark and scary — filled the auditorium.

Then a deep voice boomed over the PA system: "Beware! We, the demons of the Kingdom of Giljarri, unleash the Great and Powerful Theopolis!"

There was one more flash of lightning, and one more great clap of thunder, and there in the middle of the stage appeared Theopolis himself. He wore a long, shining black robe with a hood up over his head. He threw out his arms and threw his head back, so the hood flipped off.

The kids from Blackstone went crazy cheering.

"Wow," Charlie said. "You'd think they were all big fans or something."

Ty was on his feet, clapping like mad. "After an entrance like that, who wouldn't be?" he said, eyes on the stage.

Charlie shrugged. He didn't think it was such a big deal. Anyone could use a smoke machine and similar special effects. He wanted to see some impressive illusions. Then he'd be a fan.

The first few magic tricks Theopolis performed were nothing special. He sawed his assistant in half, levitated a piano, and produced a demon from the "Kingdom of Giljarri." Charlie could tell how each was done, even from way up in the balcony.

"For my finale," Theopolis announced, "I will need a volunteer."

Hands shot up all over the theater. Ty jumped to his feet and waved wildly.

"How are you going to volunteer from way up here?" Charlie said.

"Oh yeah," Ty said. He sat down.

"I'm told," Theopolis said, "that there is a large group from the local middle school here today." The kids from Blackstone cheered and hollered. Theopolis smiled at them. "Perhaps one of you would make a good volunteer," he said. "Perhaps . . . you!"

He pointed at a boy right in the middle of the large group of kids. Charlie recognized the boy, but didn't know his name.

"Lucky kid," Ty said. "Man, I can't wait to talk to him about this at school on Monday."

"You know him?" Charlie asked.

Ty nodded. "Yeah," he said. "I gave him the flyer yesterday. His name's Paul Juke. It was funny, actually. He was the only kid I gave a flyer to who already knew about the show."

On the stage, Theopolis and Paul watched as two stagehands — both dressed in hooded robes — wheeled out a huge wardrobe. They placed it in the center of the stage, right up against the heavy black curtain. The wardrobe was made of wood and looked older than the hotel.

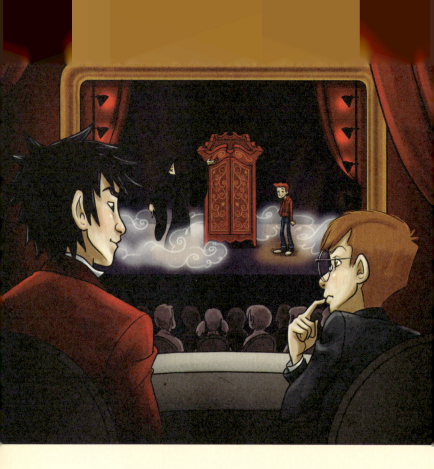

Charlie rolled his eyes. "I've seen this
wardrobe," he said. "That's the same
wardrobe they used in the 1950s. It has a
false bottom, and it's over the trapdoor.
Brack showed me the other day."

"Quiet!" Ty said. "Don't ruin the trick."

"This wardrobe," Theopolis announced from the stage in his booming, demonic voice, "was used during the last show, fifty years ago. Back then, they put in a volunteer, closed the door, and said a few magic words. The person inside would disappear."

The crowd oohed and ahhed.

"But today, I'll be doing things a little differently," Theopolis said. "Anyone can open a trapdoor. But for today's performances, I've had the trapdoors in this stage nailed closed."

Charlie leaned forward.

"I will make this boy, this brave volunteer, truly vanish," Theopolis said. "This will be no illusion. It will be real magic — magic I learned from the demons of Giljarri."

Paul stepped into the wardrobe. Theopolis closed the door behind him. He locked it with a key, and slipped the key into a pocket in his robe.

He pulled on his hood, and the lights dimmed. Smoke flowed across the stage floor. The demon voices cackled and boomed. Theopolis muttered words in a language no one could understand.

"The boy is ours now," said the deep voices. Thunder clapped and lightning streaked across the theater.

Suddenly the stage lights came back up. Theopolis pulled off his hood.

"It is done," he said, pulling the key from his pocket. "Behold!"

He opened the wardrobe.

Paul was gone.

The crowd went wild.

Theopolis stepped up to the edge of the stage and bowed deeply several times.

When the cheering died down, he put up his arms and announced, "Thank you for coming. Good night." As he spoke, the hooded stagehands returned. They wheeled the wardrobe away.

A confused murmur ran across the theater. "Where is the boy?" voices said. "Isn't he going to bring him back?"

"My friends, my friends," Theopolis said, trying to calm the crowd. Charlie noticed he was smiling. "I will produce the boy at the evening show."

The houselights came up, and Theopolis dashed backstage.

"That was weird," Ty said. "And I think you have to admit, it was also pretty amazing."

Charlie frowned. "Let's go check it out," he said. "Something's fishy with this guy."

"Of course something's fishy with this guy," Ty said. "He's a demon master!"

Charlie rolled his eyes. "Let's go," he said, tugging on Ty's maroon sleeve.

"Fine," Ty said. "Just make sure no one from school sees us hanging out together."

The boys hurried down to the stage level and, as the crowd slowly filed out, they climbed onto the stage. "Hey, who's that over there?" asked Charlie. Some kids were half-hidden in the shadows just offstage.

"They're just some of your nerd friends from the A/V Club," said Ty. "Annie said they asked to film the show for a school project."

"They're not nerds," Charlie said. "They're geeks. There's a difference: geeks are smarter."

"Whatever," said Ty. "Your geek friends, then."

Charlie rolled his eyes. Then he quickly found the trapdoor in the stage — the one they used to use for disappearing acts like this one. Rows of shiny nailheads marked the sides.

"Look," Charlie said, squatting near the trapdoor. "He wasn't lying. It really has been nailed shut."

Ty stood next to Charlie and crossed his arms. "There's no mystery here," he said. "The Great Theopolis is a real magician."

Charlie stood and shook his head. "I'll figure it out," he said, looking around, "and I'll start with that wardrobe. Where is it?"

"The stagehands probably would have put it back in storage, under the stage," Ty said. "Follow me."

In the center of the big, dusty, musty under-stage space was the wardrobe they were looking for.

Charlie pulled open the doors. It was very big — bigger than he could have guessed from the balcony. The inside was blond wood, unlike the outside, which had been painted red with gold trim.

"What are we looking for?" Ty said.

"First of all, Paul," Charlie said.

"He's not inside," Ty said. "Now what?"

Charlie didn't answer. He felt around the box, looking for secret doors or handles or anything. On the floor of the wardrobe, he found a hidden switch. The floor snapped and swung down, but not all the way.

"If this were over the trapdoor in the stage, it would open all the way," Charlie said.

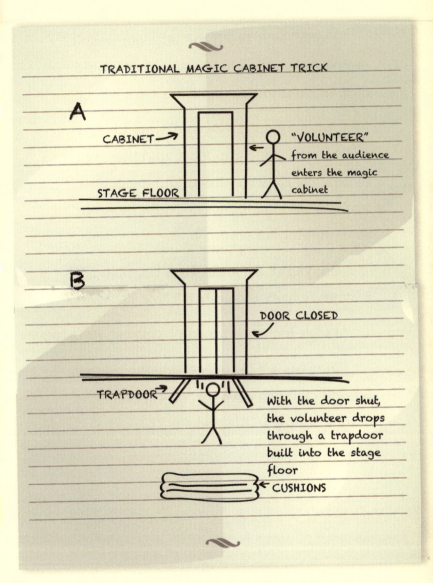

TRADITIONAL MAGIC CABINET TRICK

A

CABINET →

"VOLUNTEER" from the audience enters the magic cabinet

STAGE FLOOR

B

DOOR CLOSED

TRAPDOOR →

With the door shut, the volunteer drops through a trapdoor built into the stage floor

CUSHIONS

"Right," said Ty. "If the trapdoor wasn't nailed down. Then the person inside could drop down into this room."

Charlie nodded. "Of course, we already checked the stage trapdoors, and they were sealed," he said. He stared into the open wardrobe. "Something's not right here," he said, tapping his chin.

"Uh, yeah," Ty said. "Paul is missing. It's why we're here, remember?"

"That's not what I mean," Charlie said.

But he didn't finish his thought, because a hand clamped down on his shoulder and a light flashed in his eyes.

# Joey Bingham, Reporter

"Perfect!" said . . . someone. Charlie couldn't see well enough yet to know who.

"Who are you?" Ty asked.

Charlie squinted. Ty rubbed his eyes.

"Oh, sorry about the flash," said a young man. He held a big, old-fashioned camera. "It's just too dark down here to shoot without it."

"Why are you taking our picture?" Charlie asked.

"Well, I wanted a good shot of the magic wardrobe," the man said. "Having a couple of kids in the picture seemed like good idea, for that human-interest angle."

"Uh, okay," Ty said.

The young man smiled. "I'm Joey Bingham, by the way," he said. "I'm a reporter for Channel Fifty."

"I thought I recognized you," Ty said.

"Recognized him?" Charlie said. "I can still hardly see him." He rubbed at his eyes with his fists.

Bingham let the camera hang from a strap around his neck. Then he picked up another camera that was also hanging from his neck. This time, it was a video camera. He switched it on. "Did you boys know the missing boy?" Bingham asked in a deep newscaster voice.

"Wait, are you filming us?" Ty asked, backing away.

"Of course," Bingham said. He followed Ty with the camera. "Don't you want to be on TV?"

"No!" Ty said, hurrying behind the wardrobe. "Especially not with Hitchcock. It'll ruin my reputation."

"Hitchcock? You mean like the scary movie director?" asked Bingham.

Charlie nodded. He sometimes got tired of having to explain his last name to people.

"That could be an angle for my story," said Bingham. "It's just like a Hitchcock film. Some unsuspecting person disappears, and then —"

"Uh, he's a student at Blackstone Middle School," Charlie said as the reporter pointed the camera at him. "The kid who disappeared, I mean. I don't know him, though. Paul something."

"Paul Juke," Ty said, jumping out from behind the wardrobe. "His name's Paul Juke. He's in my technology class."

"Great," Bingham said. "Let's get something out to the station. They can have an interview on the air in two minutes."

"An interview?" Charlie said. "Just because of a magic trick?"

"Of course!" said Theopolis in his booming voice.

Everyone turned to look as the magician came into the storage room, still wearing his mysterious black robe. "Because this was no simple magic trick."

Bingham excitedly turned the little video camera on himself. "This is Joey Bingham with an exclusive story," he said. "We have here the magician himself, the master of demons, the man responsible for the missing boy's magical disappearance."

Then Bingham crouched in front of Theopolis and aimed the camera at him. "Mr. Theopolis," the reporter said. "Tell us: where is the boy?"

Theopolis smiled. "I can produce the boy at any time," he said. "I am in complete control of the shift that has occurred for the boy."

"The what?" Ty said.

Theopolis fixed him with an evil glare. "The demons under my power can alter space and time," he said in a rough whisper. "If I so desire, they will take a piece of our space and time and move it to another space and time. That is what they've done."

"And you can bring him back any time?" Charlie asked.

Theopolis nodded gravely.

"Then do it," Charlie said.

Theopolis threw his head back and laughed. Bingham was getting the whole thing on video. "I will, young man," the magician said. "At tonight's performance. Then the world will see that I am the greatest — and indeed, the first ever — real, true magician in history!"

# Proof

"This is ridiculous," Charlie said.

He and Ty were in the office behind the
front desk of the Abracadabra Hotel with
Annie Solo, the girl who often worked at the
check-in desk.

Ty leaned back in the big chair in
the corner. "I don't know, Hitchcock," he
said. He put his hands behind his head.
"Theopolis is pretty amazing. He proved he
can do real magic."

"He did not," Charlie insisted.

Annie nodded. "He did," she said, still
staring at the TV. The news was showing
Joey Bingham's interview with Theopolis for
the fifth time that afternoon. "He nailed the
trapdoor shut. It had to be demons."

"Shifts in space and time," Ty said.

Charlie rolled his eyes.

"I think it's real," Annie said. "I think
it wasn't a trick at all. I think it was real
magic. I truly believe that."

"You're crazy," Charlie said.

"I'm with Annie," Ty said. "Am I crazy
too?"

Charlie swallowed. They might have been becoming friends, but Ty was still the scariest kid in eighth grade. He decided to ignore the question.

"Prove us wrong, Charlie," Annie said.

"That's my plan," he said, standing up. "Come on, Ty."

"Why should I?" Ty asked, leaning back in his chair.

"I don't know, in the name of truth?" Charlie suggested. "Because uncovering mysteries in this hotel is what we do?"

Ty crossed his arms and stared at Charlie.

"Because I helped you solve two mysteries already, so you owe me?" Charlie said. He grinned sheepishly.

"He's got you there," Annie said. "If not for Charlie, you'll never get that bike you've had your eye on."

Charlie smiled at Annie. The Slamhammer, which Ty was really close to being able to buy, would convince him.

"Fine," Ty said. "Where do we start?"

"Theopolis's room," Charlie said. "Come on. Let's go."

\* \* \*

"Why, hello, Master Hitchcock, and Master Yu. Where are you two headed?" Brack asked as Charlie and Ty stepped into his elevator.

"To see Mr. Theopolis," Charlie said.

"Thirteenth floor," Brack said. "Yes."

"It's so weird that he's on the thirteenth floor," Ty said. "No one stays on the thirteenth floor!"

"Why not?" Charlie asked as the elevator started its slow climb.

Brack shrugged. "It's an old tradition, and lots of old-time magicians are very superstitious," he said. "They believe the number thirteen is bad luck."

"It is," Ty said.

"They say the number itself has bad magic in it," Brack went on. He pulled out his watch again. "I always thought it had something to do with time."

He popped open the watch. "The last hour of the day is twelve," he explained, pointing at the watch face. "Perhaps a thirteenth hour seems unnatural, and so the number seems unnatural."

The old man turned to face Ty. "Have a close look," he said. He held out the watch to Ty, and Ty leaned close.

"Yup," he said. "Just like every other watch. It goes up to tw—"

But he was cut off, because suddenly a fine stream of water squirted from the center of the watch face, soaking Ty's face.

"Hey!" Ty said, covering his face. "What gives?"

Charlie couldn't help laughing. "Good trick, Brack," he said. "But — I looked closely at your watch earlier today. It was definitely not a joke watch. I could tell from the shine that it was real old metal."

"Indeed," Brack said.

He reached into the pocket of his coat and produced the real watch. The two were nearly identical. Anyone would have been fooled. "I had this one made special," Brack said, "just so my two watches — the real antique one and the other fake, practical-joke one — would look almost exactly alike. Only an expert — or you, Mr. Hitchcock — would be able to tell them apart."

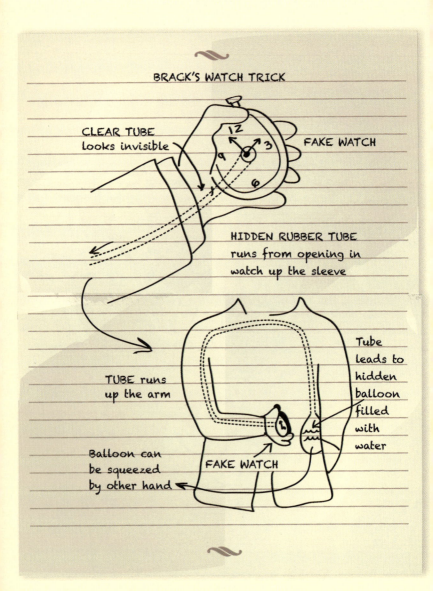

BRACK'S WATCH TRICK

CLEAR TUBE
looks invisible

FAKE WATCH

HIDDEN RUBBER TUBE
runs from opening in
watch up the sleeve

Tube
leads to
hidden
balloon
filled
with
water

TUBE runs
up the arm

FAKE WATCH

Balloon can
be squeezed
by other hand

The old man giggled as the door opened on the thirteenth floor. "In fact, I've squirted my own face more than once by accident," he said. "Anyway, here you are."

"Thanks a lot, Brack," Ty said, wiping his face.

"Yeah, thanks," said Charlie, and the boys stepped out.

The hallway was completely dark. "Hey, is this right?" Charlie asked. "The lights are all off!" He turned back to the elevator, but the doors were closed, and the elevator was already heading back down to the lobby.

# Room 1307

"Let's go," Ty said. "Theopolis is in room 1305, I think."

"Isn't it weird that it's so dark here?" Charlie asked.

Ty shrugged. "Not really," he said. "I mean, no one but Theopolis is staying here."

"No one else is staying on the floor?" Charlie asked. They walked slowly down the dark hall. Only some sunlight, coming in the windows at the far ends of the hall, offered any light at all.

"Theopolis requested this floor," said Ty. "Otherwise we'd never even bother offering it. Everyone insists on staying somewhere else. I told you. Magicians are superstitious."

"Why would he ask for it?" Charlie said.

"According to Annie, he said the floor has a lot of power," Ty said. "Power he would harness for his magic."

Charlie rolled his eyes. "Oh, that makes sense," he muttered.

"Here we are," Ty said. "Room 1305."

Room 1305 was a corner room. Some light showed under the door. Charlie knocked. "Mr. Theopolis?" he said.

The door swung open.

"It is I!" Theopolis declared grandly. "The Great and Powerful Theopolis!" He raised his arms toward the ceiling.

Ty and Charlie looked at each other. Abruptly, Theopolis lowered his arms and looked behind them.

"Mr. Bingham, from the news show, isn't with you?" he asked. The boys shook their heads.

"Oh," said the magician. Then he went to the couch and sat down.

He grabbed the remote for the TV and starting clicking through the channels. "Come on in, then. Did you need something?" he asked.

"We were, uh, hoping to look around," Charlie said. "We, uh —"

"We work here," Ty chimed in. "So, you know, we need to make sure everything's going all right. You know, with the hotel stay."

"You mean the missing boy?" Theopolis asked, grinning a little. "Look all you want. You won't find anything. But keep it down. I'm trying to watch bowling in here."

He picked up a bowl of chips from the table and started munching away.

It didn't take long to search the room. Charlie and Ty went over every floorboard and wall panel, looking for hidden switches and doors. They found nothing.

They met in the bedroom. "There's only one bedroom," Ty said. "That's funny."

"Why?" Charlie said quietly, so the magician in the living room wouldn't overhear.

"Well, the hotel has normal rooms, and it has suites," Ty said. "This is a suite. It has a living room, and it has a separate bedroom. But all the suites I've ever seen have two bedrooms at least."

"Hmm," Charlie said. "Maybe the thirteenth floor is different, and you never knew because you hardly ever come to the thirteenth floor. Since no one stays here, I mean."

"Maybe," Ty said.

Charlie and Ty headed back to the living room. "So, it seems like everything is on the up-and-up," Charlie said.

"If you mean you didn't find the boy, I know," said the magician, munching away at his chips. He had his feet up on the coffee table now, so his robe was a little open at the ankles. Charlie noticed he had on a pair of jeans underneath.

The Great and Powerful Theopolis didn't look so powerful now, lounging on his couch with potato chip crumbs on his chin.

The boys headed back toward the elevator. "Well, I guess that was a waste of time," Ty said. "We didn't find any clues."

"Maybe not," Charlie said, "but it's never a waste of time to investigate every possibility."

"Wait a second," Ty said, grabbing Charlie's shirt. "Listen."

Charlie held his breath. "I don't hear anything," he whispered.

"I do," Ty said. He put his ear to the wall. "It sounds like a TV is on."

Charlie listened at the wall too. "Now I hear it," he said. "But it's probably just Theopolis. Remember? He was watching TV."

"He was watching bowling," Ty pointed out. "This sounds like . . . yup, it's *Alien Cyborg Attack Part 7*. I've seen it a hundred times. This is the part right before the Cyborgs disembark from —"

"I believe you," Charlie said. He glanced up ahead, at the door to room 1307. "It must be in there," he said. Then he knocked on the door. "Hello?"

"There's no way any guests are staying in this room," Ty said. "Annie would have told me. Theopolis is the only guy on the floor."

"Is anyone in there?" Charlie called again. There was no reply.

Ty and Charlie looked at each other and said at the same time, "Pass key!"

"It's in the office," Ty said as he stabbed the elevator-call button. "Come on."

# Empty

Ty twirled the key chain and whistled as the elevator climbed back up to the thirteenth floor. There were three of them in the elevator, but this time the third person wasn't Brack.

"Thanks for letting me tag along," said Joey Bingham. "This will be quite a scoop if the missing boy is in room 1307. The whole city is talking about Theopolis's performance."

Ty tapped the golden railing inside the elevator. "I don't understand why Brack isn't in the elevator," he said. "He's always in this elevator."

On the thirteenth floor, there was a ding, and the doors opened. The three of them stepped off the elevator. "Hello!" a voice said. Charlie spun around and there was Brack, standing in the open doors of another elevator.

"Hello," he said, smiling. "I guess I'm not quite where you expected me to be, huh?"

"What are you up to, Brack?" Charlie asked.

"Nothing, nothing," said Brack. "There's more than one elevator in this hotel. Sometimes I like to check out the others. Get a different view on things. Good luck with your case." He slipped back into his usual elevator, closed the doors, and was off.

The boys and the reporter rushed to room 1307. The sound of the movie was gone. "Totally quiet now," Ty said as he fumbled with the pass key. He opened the door and the three of them rushed in . . .

. . . and tripped over the coffee table in the total darkness.

"Watch it!" Ty said.

"Who's on my head?" Charlie squealed.

"Get off my camera!" shouted Bingham.

Ty managed to reach a lamp and switch it on. "I'd say there's no one staying in this room," he said.

It was completely clean. No one's bags were there, no towels had been used, and the beds were made. Charlie noticed there were two bedrooms in this suite, unlike Theopolis's.

Ty picked up the room phone and waited a moment. "Annie," he said. "Has anyone checked into room 1307 recently?" He didn't have to wait long for a reply. "Thanks," he said, and hung up. "Like I said. No one. She didn't even have to look it up. No one ever stays on this floor."

"Besides Theopolis," Charlie said. "But why him?"

"Because of the power," Ty said. "Like I told you."

"Okay, okay, the power of the thirteenth floor," Charlie said, trying not to roll his eyes, "but what other normal human reason might he have?"

The reporter snapped his fingers. "No prying eyes!" he said. "And no eavesdroppers."

"Exactly what I was thinking," Charlie said. "It would be easy to hide the boy on this floor, but on another floor someone might notice."

"So let's look around," Ty said. "Maybe he moved him, and the TV will be on in some other room."

But the three didn't make it more than a few feet from room 1307 before there was a great flash of light, a booming crash like thunder, and the deep evil cackle they had begun to associate with Theopolis's magic.

At the end of the hall, in front of the door to the emergency stairs and the ice machine, there appeared — in a billowing cloud of smoke — a demon.

The demon was huge and purple and muscular, with great twirling horns on its head, and huge claws and cloven feet. Its tail swung violently behind it.

"Who dares disturb Theopolis?" the demon bellowed, its voice echoing through the dark halls of the thirteenth floor.

"We're sorry!" Bingham said. He dropped to his knees and covered his face. "Please don't hurt us!"

"You must stay off this floor!" the demon shouted. The walls seemed to shake. "The thirteenth floor is rich with power, but it can destroy simple mortals like you!"

Ty, Charlie, and Bingham sprinted for the elevators. They stabbed at the call button. "Come on, come on!" Ty said. "Hurry, Brack!"

But Charlie stopped. "Wait a second," he said. "What are we, little kids?"

He turned and looked at the demon. It hadn't moved. It still roared and cackled. Thunder still clapped and lightning still crashed across the ceiling. "These are the same special effects Theopolis used on stage," Charlie said. "Are we going to let him scare us away so easily?"

He stomped back up the hall toward the demon. Ty and Bingham stayed behind him.

"Who dares disturb Theopolis?" the demon growled.

"That's the same thing it said before," Charlie said. "It's on a loop, I bet. If I can find the projector, I can just switch it off."

A hand clamped on his shoulder.

"Do not approach the demon!" a deep voice said.

Charlie spun around and was faced by Theopolis himself.

"Didn't you hear the great beast's warning?" the magician roared. "He protects me at all costs. He is far more powerful than you could possibly imagine! You must run from this place and never come back!"

Charlie smirked at him and shrugged. Then he walked right up to the demon. He reached around in the smoke until he found a rectangular device. He found a power cord and followed it to the wall. Then he unplugged it.

The demon vanished. The smoke settled and began to disappear. The thunder was silenced, and the lightning flashes stopped.

Charlie turned back to the hallway, holding the end of the power cord in his hand. "How do you explain this, Theopolis?" he asked.

But there was no reply. The magician had vanished.

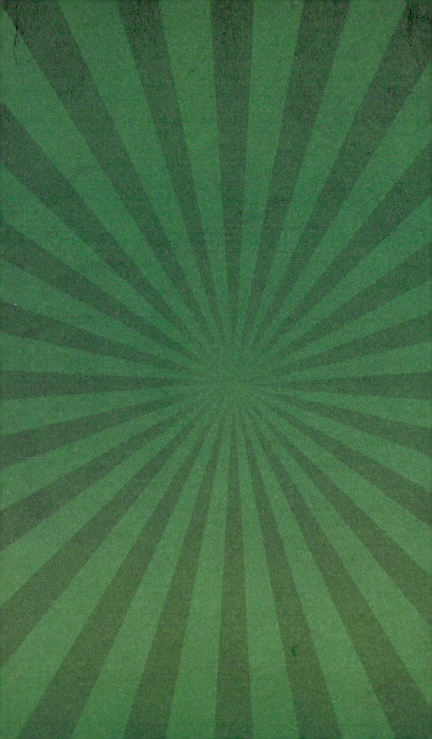

# The Black Stamp

"I'm certain Paul is on the thirteenth floor someplace," Charlie said, back in the lobby. "It's the quietest floor in the hotel, and we heard someone watching that movie. *Space Mutants Invade Part Ten*, or whatever."

"Ooh, I love that movie," Annie Solo said. She took a bite of her cherry licorice whip. "Remember that part when the alien with five tentacles bit the head off the —"

"Kind of getting off track here," Charlie said. "We have a mystery to solve, remember?"

Annie shrugged. "Maybe you do," she said. "But I don't."

"You don't still think Theopolis is a real magician, do you?" Charlie asked. "Not after the special effects show we told you about."

"Just because the big demon upstairs was fake, that doesn't mean that Paul's disappearance was fake too," Annie said.

Before Charlie could argue, Ty jumped in.

"Maybe we should take another look at that wardrobe," he said. "The one Theopolis used for the trick."

"We looked at it already," Charlie said.

"Yeah, I know," Ty said. "And you said something seemed wrong. But you never figured out what."

"It's worth a try," Charlie said.

* * *

Back under the stage, the crews were already moving things around for the evening performance.

"I hope the wardrobe is still here," Charlie said. "It'll be way trickier to sneak a look at it if it's already upstairs for the show."

Two stagehands were standing nearby. "You mean Theopolis's wardrobe?" one of them asked.

Charlie said, "That's the one. You know where it is?"

Both stagehands nodded toward the corner. "There it is," said one. "That goofball Theopolis won't let anyone move it but him."

"That's okay with us," the other stagehand added. "That thing looks heavy."

"Thanks," Charlie said. Then the stagehands walked away.

"Looks the same to me," Ty said once Charlie had opened the wardrobe's doors.

"Me too," Charlie said. He tried the false bottom, and it opened. Everything was just how he remembered it. He climbed right inside and tapped on every surface.

"What's that?" Ty asked, pointing at a black stain on the back inner wall of the wardrobe.

Charlie squinted at the stain.

"It looks printed," he said. "I think it's the logo and company name of the manufacturer. It says, 'Hockney and Sons. 1935.'"

"Wow," Ty said. "That thing is really old-time, like Brack."

Charlie tapped his chin. "Hmm. Brack . . . time . . . " he said quietly. Then he snapped his fingers. "Brack's watch! That's it!"

"His watch?" Ty said. "The squirting one?"

Charlie nodded. "I have a phone call to make," he said. "Come on."

# Video Proof

"Thanks for coming down and setting this up so quickly," Charlie said. He was back in the office behind the front desk again. Sitting in the various chairs and couches were Annie, Ty, and Bingham.

At the front of the room, fiddling with cables and a wide-screen monitor, was Kyle Bukowski, president of the Blackstone Middle School A/V club.

"It's no problem," Kyle said. "I'm always happy to help with an audio/video emergency. In a moment, I'll have all nine videos that we shot of Theopolis's performance cued up for us."

Kyle plugged in a few things, pushed a couple of buttons, and it was done. On the monitor popped up nine moving images, each in its own section.

Each little video showed a different angle of Theopolis's performance.

They watched the whole vanishing act a couple of times.

"What are we looking for, exactly?" Ty asked.

Charlie watched the videos until he saw just the right frame. "Kyle, can you pause it right there," Charlie said, "so we have a clear view of the inside of the wardrobe?"

"Sure," Kyle said. He paused one of the nine videos, and then zoomed in. "How's this?"

"Perfect," Charlie said. He pointed at the inside of the wardrobe. "Anything look funny, Ty?"

Ty squinted at the screen. "What do you mean?" he asked.

"Look at the inside back wall," Charlie said. He leaned back in the big chair. "What's not there?"

Ty squinted. He leaned in closer and closer to the monitor, until his nose practically touched the screen. Then his eyes went wide. "The black stamp!" he said.

Charlie smiled and said, "Hockney and Sons. 1935."

"Did you know that wouldn't be there?" Ty asked.

"Wait a second," said Bingham. "Who's Hockney?"

"I'll explain later," Charlie said. "First we have to find that wardrobe." He pointed at the one on the monitor.

"That's not the real wardrobe?" Annie asked.

"Nope," Charlie said. "Not at all."

"So where's the real one?" Ty said.

"Probably somewhere he could keep a close eye on it," Charlie said, "and where no one would be likely to stumble upon it."

He and Ty thought for a moment, and it came to them at the very same time.

Together they said, "The thirteenth floor!"

"But where?" Annie said. "You two have already checked his room, and you roamed the halls. It couldn't be in another room, because he wouldn't have a key to any other rooms."

Charlie smiled at Ty. "Remember how you said every suite has at least two bedrooms?" he said. "I have a hunch about where the second bedroom in Theopolis's room has disappeared to."

"What are you talking about?" asked Ty.

"Before I answer that," said Charlie, "we should go talk to Brack."

Ty squinted at him. "You think he might have seen something?" he asked.

"Yeah, if he's been checking out the other elevators," Charlie said. "He might have seen a couple of men pushing a wardrobe."

# The Closet

The thirteenth floor was even darker and creepier than it had been earlier that day.

Demonic laughter filled the hallway. The floors creaked, even when no one was walking. Every so often, up ahead or just out of sight, something would flicker across, like a shadowy figure.

"More of Theopolis's tricks," Charlie said. "Don't let them frighten you."

"Who-who-who's frightened?" stammered Bingham.

"You are, for one," said Ty. "Here's his room."

The three of them stopped in front of room 1305. Charlie knocked. "Mr. Theopolis?" he said.

The door swung open. "What do you two want?" Theopolis said. "Haven't you bothered me enough?"

"The reporter is with us this time," Charlie said.

Theopolis's eyes lit up. "Then enter if you dare!" he shouted.

Charlie and Ty rolled their eyes, and the three visitors walked in.

"Okay, Ty," said Charlie as Bingham began filming. "If this were a regular two-bedroom suite, where would the second bedroom be?"

Ty looked around, and his face wrinkled with the strain. "I think," he said, turning slowly in the living room, "right there."

He stopped and pointed at the closet doors. They were tall and black, like the polished top keys of a piano. In fact, much of the room was decorated with the same black finish.

Charlie strode to the closet and pulled open the doors. The inside of the closet was very familiar. Bright blond wood.

"It looks exactly like the wardrobe," Ty said.

"Except for one thing that's missing," Charlie said. "The stamp."

"Do not go into that closet!" Theopolis bellowed. He ran and got between the boys and the closet. "There is great and terrible power in there! I can't be held responsible for what might happen!"

"Wait," Ty said. "Do you hear that? It sounds like another movie. In fact, I'm pretty sure it's *Alien Cyborg Attack Part Eight*."

Charlie smiled. Then he walked right into the closet. He tapped the back wall, and it instantly sprung open.

"A false back," Charlie said. "Just as I thought. And the TV we heard was coming from through here, not room 1307 at all."

Charlie stepped through the opening, right into the second bedroom. It had been hidden behind the wardrobe, and the wardrobe had been disguised as a simple closet.

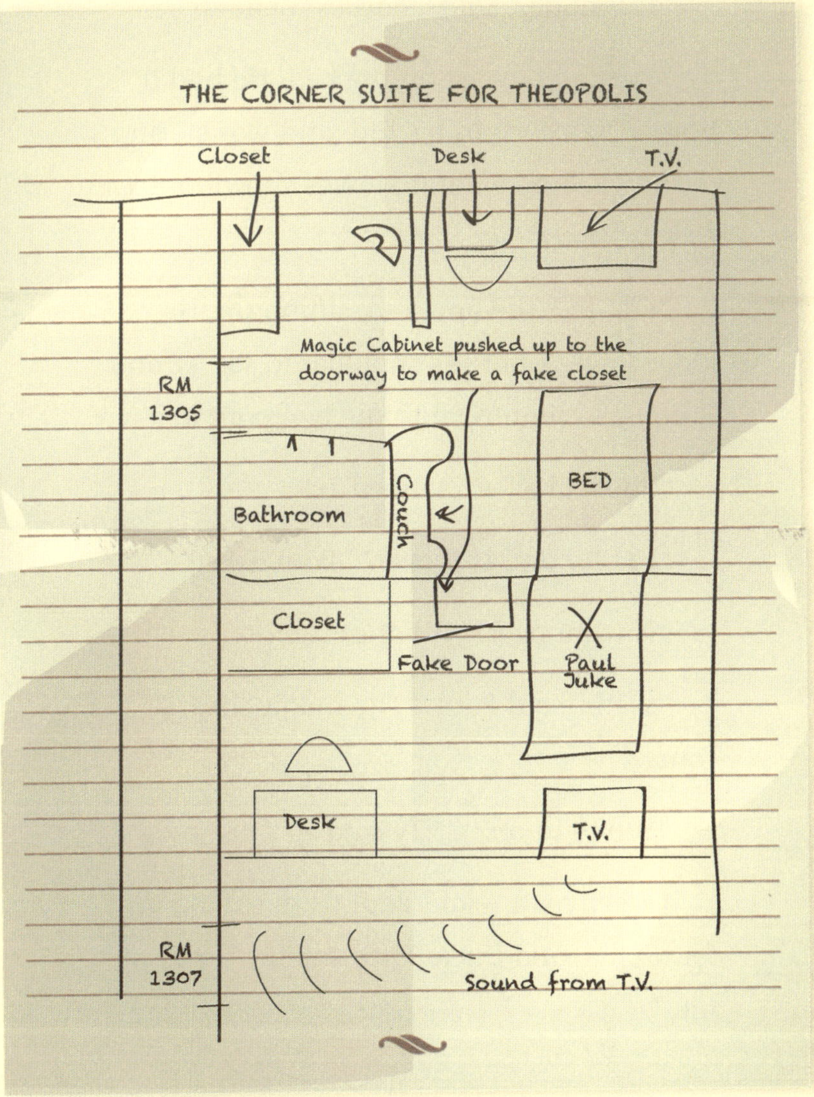

# THE CORNER SUITE FOR THEOPOLIS

Closet

Desk

T.V.

Magic Cabinet pushed up to the
doorway to make a fake closet

RM
1305

Couch

BED

Bathroom

Closet

Fake Door

Paul
Juke

Desk

T.V.

RM
1307

Sound from T.V.

"It is done," said Charlie. "Behold!"

A young boy sat on the bed. He had a bowl of popcorn in his lap, and was staring at the TV. Sure enough, it was showing *Alien Cyborg Attack Part Eight.*

"Oh, hi," the boy said, sitting up. He looked over Charlie's shoulder to see Ty and Bingham climbing into the bedroom too.

"Paul Juke!" exclaimed Ty.

"Hi, Ty. Um, is it over?" Paul asked.

"Is what over?" Bingham said.

"Well," said Paul. "The magic trick, of course."

"You're in on it?" Ty said.

"Well, yeah," said Paul. "I'm saving up for a bike, and Uncle Theo said he'd pay me."

# The Big Finale

"This is Joey Bingham for Action 50 News," the reporter said, grinning at his own camera. "I'm at the Abracadabra Hotel, where the Great Theopolis is about to use magic to bring back the boy who vanished at the noon show."

The house was packed. Everyone who had gone to the day show was back, and so were loads of people who had seen Bingham's earlier reports about the missing boy.

"Are you sure about this?" Charlie whispered. He sat with Ty on an overturned crate under the stage. They were going to help with the big finish Theopolis had promised. "We can still reveal the truth. We figured out that Theopolis isn't a true magician, like he claims."

"We could do that," Ty said. "We could also enjoy all the publicity for this show, for the hotel, and for the theater. This is going to do wonders for the Abracadabra Hotel."

"I suppose," Charlie said.

"Besides, you convinced me and Annie, right?" Ty said. "And that was the point."

Charlie nodded. Just then, one of the stagehands popped his head in the door. "Everyone ready down here?" he asked.

"We're ready," replied Ty.

Paul got up from his seat against the wall. "Finally," he said. He stepped up onto the overturned crate between Ty and Charlie. "Uncle Theo owes me big time."

Charlie and Ty stood and clasped their hands together. "Ready?" asked Ty.

"One," they all said together, "two, three!" And with a great grunt, Paul was launched up and through the open trapdoor, into the wardrobe on the stage—the original wardrobe, with the false bottom and stamp that said "Hockney and Sons. 1935."

Charlie and Ty sat back down and waited. Seconds later, they heard the crowd above burst into cheers and applause.

"I guess it went well," Charlie said.

"And you know what it means when the hotel does well, and I've helped," said Ty.

Charlie nodded. "Yup," he said.

"A raise," said Ty. "And that brings me one step closer to my Tezuki Slamhammer 750, Edition 6, in cherry-pop lightning red."

"I guess when you get the bike you won't need my help anymore," Charlie said. "Right?"

Ty shrugged. "I don't know," he said. "I mean, there's always a new mystery at the Abracadabra."

"Which reminds me," Charlie said. "Isn't Brack planning another huge magic show?"

"Indeed I am," a voice said. But when the boys turned to look, Brack was nowhere to be found.

# ABOUT THE AUTHOR

**MICHAEL DAHL** grew up reading everything he could find about his hero Harry Houdini, and worked as a magician's assistant when he was a teenager. Even though he cannot disappear, he is very good at escaping things. Dahl has written the popular Library of Doom series, the Dragonblood books, and the Finnegan Zwake series. He currently lives in the Midwest in a haunted house.

# ABOUT THE ILLUSTRATOR

**LISA K. WEBER** is an illustrator currently living in Oakland, California. She graduated from Parsons School of Design in 2000 and then began freelancing. Since then, she has completed many print, animation, and design projects, including graphic novelizations of classic literature, character and background designs for children's cartoons, and textiles for dog clothing.

# DISCUSSION QUESTIONS

**1.** Explain Theopolis's trick. How did he do it?

**2.** Have you seen a magic show? Talk about some of the tricks you saw.

**3.** Would you want to stay at the Abracadabra Hotel? Why or why not?

# WRITING PROMPTS

**1.** Try writing one of the chapters in this book from Brack's point of view. How does the story change? What does Brack see, hear, think, and feel?

**2.** Create your own magic trick. What is it? How does it work?

**3.** Paul Juke's uncle is a magician. Write about someone you know who has a very interesting job. What does he or she do? What makes that job interesting?

# GLOSSARY

**deny** (di-NYE)—say that something isn't true

**exclusive** (ek-SKLOO-siv)—a story that appears in one place only

**finale** (fuh-NAL-ee)—the last part of a show

**founder** (FOUND-ur)—the person who set up or started something

**illusion** (i-LOO-zhuhn)—something that appears to exist but does not; a trick

**namesake** (NAYM-sayk)—the person for whom someone or something is named

**photographic** (foh-tuh-GRAF-ik)—if someone has a photographic memory, they remember things in great detail

**refurbished** (ri-FUR-bishd)—fixed up and made to seem new

**stagehand** (STAYJ-hand)—a person who works behind the scenes at a theater

**superstitious** (soo-pur-STISH-uhss)—believing in bad luck

**unnatural** (uhn-NACH-ur-uhl)—not usual or normal

# WHERE'S ROVER?

**M**ental magic can help you read people's minds, make predictions, or put a puzzle together. And with this astounding trick, it can even help you find a lost dog!

---

**You need:** Three cups, a small toy dog, a secret assistant, and a table

---

## PERFORMANCE:

**1.** First, show the toy dog and the cups to the audience, then set the props on the table. Tell the audience you have a special mental connection with the dog. Say, "Rover is my special pal. I can find him even if he gets lost under the cups."

**2.** Next, ask your secret assistant, who is sitting in the audience, to come and help you with this trick. Then turn your back to the table. Ask your secret assistant to place the toy dog under one of the cups and mix them up.

**3.** Turn back to the table when your assistant is done. Then begin pretending to use your mental powers to see which cup the dog is under. You will be able to find the correct cup by looking at your secret assistant's feet.

**4.** If the dog is under the left cup, your assistant's foot will point to the left.

If the dog is under the center cup, your assistant's feet both point forward.

If the dog is under the right cup, your assistant's foot will point to the right.

**5.** Once you know where the toy dog is, lift up the cup to reveal the toy. The audience will be stunned by your awesome mental powers!

Like this trick? Learn more in the book *Amazing Magic Tricks: Apprentice Level* by Norm Barnhart!
All images and text © 2009 Capstone Press. Used by permission.

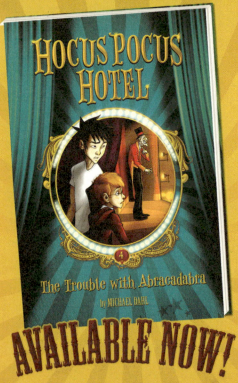